THREE-STAR BILLY

★ ★ ★

PAT HUTCHINS

Greenwillow Books, New York

Gouache paints were used for the full-color art.
The text type is Benguiat.

Printed in Hong Kong by South China Printing
Company (1988) Ltd.

First Edition   10 9 8 7 6 5 4 3 2

★   ★   ★

Library of Congress Cataloging-in-Publication Data
Hutchins, Pat (date)
Three-star Billy / by Pat Hutchins.
p.   cm.
Summary: Billy, a bad-tempered little monster
who does not want to be in nursery school, throws
tantrums that only result in his teacher's giving him
praise and three stars.
ISBN 0-688-13078-X (trade).
ISBN 0-688-13079-8 (lib. bdg.)
(1. Nursery schools—Fiction.   2. Schools—Fiction.
3. Behavior—Fiction.   4. Monsters—Fiction.)
I. Title.   II. Title: 3-star Billy.
PZ7.H9616525Th   1994
(E)—dc20
93-26517   CIP   AC

For Ron, Margaret, Chris, Anna, Joby,
Richard, Fiona, and Maisie Maris

BILLY didn't want to go to nursery school.

"You'll like it," said Ma and Pa.

"And if you're good," said Hazel, "you might get a star."

"Hello, Billy," said Teacher.
"I'm sure you will be a good little monster."
But Billy didn't want to be good.

Teacher said they could do some painting.

But Billy didn't want to paint,
and he flung his pots of paint at the paper
and made a TERRIBLE mess.

"Look, everyone!" said Teacher.
"Billy's painting is really good!
It's the most TERRIBLE, MONSTROUS
painting I've ever seen."
And she gave Billy a star.

Teacher said they could do some singing.

But Billy didn't want to sing,
and he hollered at the top of his voice
and made a DREADFUL noise.

"Listen, everyone!" said Teacher.
"Billy's singing is really good!
It's the most DREADFUL, MONSTROUS
singing I've ever heard!"
And she gave Billy another star.

Teacher said they could do some dancing.

But Billy didn't want to dance,
and he jumped up and down and stamped
so hard that he frightened everyone.

"Just look!" said Teacher.
"See how good Billy's dancing is!
It's the most FRIGHTFUL, MONSTROUS
dancing I've ever seen!"
And she gave Billy a third star.

All the other little monsters asked Billy
to show them how to paint TERRIBLE paintings
and sing DREADFUL songs
and dance FRIGHTFUL dances.

When it was time to go home,
Hazel and Ma and Pa came to collect Billy.

But Billy didn't want to go home,
and he yelled so HORRIBLY
that he scared all the other parents.

"Just listen to that yelling!" said Teacher.
"It's really good. That's the most HORRIBLE,
MONSTROUS yelling I've ever heard."

And she promised to give Billy another star
in the morning.